The Firebird

Illustrated by Alida Massari

Retold by Mairi Mackinnon

There was once a king who lived in a splendid palace with beautiful gardens.

There were graceful trees
and sweet-scented flowers,
sparkling fountains and singing birds.

In the heart of the garden was an orchard, hidden behind a high stone wall.

Here were the king's most precious trees,
with blossoms of diamonds, rubies and pearls.

Right in the middle stood an apple tree,
and every year it bore apples of pure gold.

One morning, the king was horrified to see that one of the
golden apples was missing.

"Who dares to steal from me?" he roared.

The next night, another apple was taken, then another, and another...

"I will catch the thief," promised the king's son, Prince Ivan.

All night long he waited, until at last he saw a beautiful fiery bird, circling the orchard on delicate wings.

As she snatched at an apple, Ivan seized her long tail...

...but she struggled free, and Ivan was left clutching a single feather.

The king heard Ivan's story in amazement.
His eyes gleamed when he saw the feather.

"Bring me this Firebird!" he commanded.

Prince Ivan set out, riding deep into the snowy forests
with the Firebird's feather tucked under his cloak.

"Go back, go back," moaned the North Wind, "or the wolves will eat you!"

Suddenly a great silver wolf sprang at the prince's horse. Ivan
drove the beast away, but his poor horse collapsed onto the snow.

"I'm sorry." The wolf bowed its great head.
"I couldn't help myself... but I will make it up to you."

"How can you possibly do that?" asked Ivan bitterly.

"You must trust me," said the wolf.
"Climb on my back, and I will take you to the Firebird."

Together, they leaped into the air. High over the icy treetops
they soared, until they saw the great palace of a distant land.

"The Firebird is at the top of that tower," said Silver Wolf.

"Go now, and you will be able to take her;
but whatever you do, don't touch her cage."

In the tower room, the Firebird shone bright as the sun.
Ivan reached inside her cage, but his hand brushed the golden bars.

The Firebird screeched… and the palace guards rushed in.
Ivan was dragged before the king to explain himself.

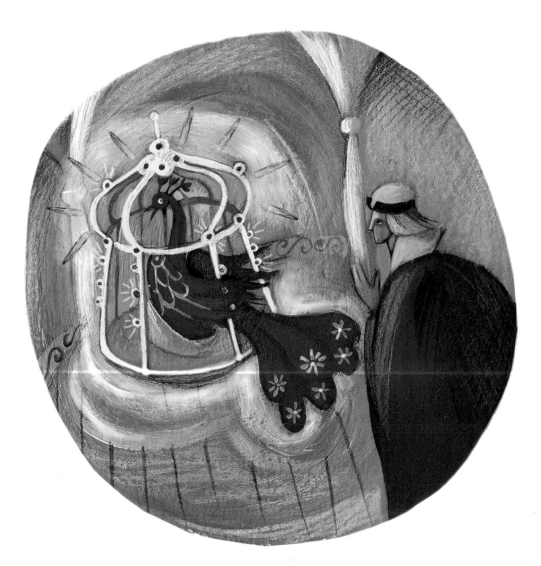

"Well then, I will let you have the Firebird," said the king at last,
"if you will bring me the winged Horse of Power."

"Hmm, the Horse of Power," said Silver Wolf.
"That's far, far away, but we can be there by nightfall."

He leaped into the air, and swooped low over the oceans to another palace.

"You'll find the horse in the furthest stable," said Silver Wolf.
"Whatever you do, don't touch her bridle."

The Horse of Power pawed the ground. Ivan reached for
a rope halter, but his sleeve brushed her glittering bridle.

The horse neighed… and the palace guards rushed in.

Once more, Ivan was dragged before the king of the land to explain himself.

"I will let you have the Horse of Power," said the king,
"but first you must do something for me."

"I have a daughter,"
the king continued.
His eyes filled with tears.

"My only child, stolen by the
wicked wizard Koshchey.

Please, brave prince,
bring her back to me."

When he heard the king's request, Silver Wolf shook his head sadly.
"Good luck, Prince Ivan. This will be your hardest task yet.

I will do all I can to help, but many have tried and failed before you."

They flew through the air until they saw a fortress on a mountain crag.

"Look, there is Koshchey's castle," said Silver Wolf.

With one last leap, Silver Wolf landed in a moonlit garden.
Twelve beautiful girls were dancing around a fountain,
watched by a princess more beautiful still.

"Quickly, come with me," urged Ivan.
"Now, before Koshchey can stop us!"

As he spoke, the sky darkened. There was a thunderclap
and the wizard appeared, surrounded by shrieking demons.

"Too late!" he snarled. "You will never defeat me until you find my soul.
And before you find my soul, I will turn you to stone!"

"Look in the hollow tree stump," rasped Silver Wolf,
but Koshchey was already muttering his spell.

Numbness and horror seeped through Ivan's body. His legs grew
heavy and cold, and his arms grew stiff, as the spell took effect.

Then the Firebird's feather fluttered down to his feet,
and the stone melted from them like frost in the sun.

Silver Wolf leaped at Koshchey, clawing aside the howling demons.
Ivan ran to the tree stump and pulled out a box.

Inside was a gleaming golden egg. Ivan gasped.
This must be Koshchey's soul.

As Koshchey battled with Silver Wolf,
Ivan flung the egg to the ground,
where it smashed into a thousand pieces.

There was a scream of fury, and then silence.
The wizard and his demons had vanished.

"At last! He's gone..." breathed the princess.
Ivan looked around, hardly believing his eyes.

Then they heard a rumbling and a roaring,
and the castle came crashing to the ground.

"Come," said Silver Wolf. "It's time for you both to go home."

The princess and her father wept for joy to see each other again.

Then the princess took Ivan's hand. "Father..." she began.

"Ah, I understand," said the king.
"Brave prince, will you marry my daughter?"

After the wedding feast, they set out to deliver the Horse of Power.

Finally, Silver Wolf carried Ivan, the princess and the Firebird
together to Ivan's homeland.

In the starry sky, the Firebird blazed like a comet;
but all the old king wanted was to see his son, alive and well.

"I was a greedy fool," he said. "I shall set the Firebird free.
Now you are back, I know that I have the most precious thing of all."

The Firebird is one of the best-known and best-loved Russian folk tales. Many different versions of the story are told, and one inspired a famous ballet with music by Igor Stravinsky.

Edited by Lesley Sims

Designed by Lenka Hrehova

First published in 2015 by Usborne Publishing Ltd., Usborne House, 83-85 Saffron Hill, London EC1N 8RT, England. www.usborne.com Copyright © 2015 Usborne Publishing Ltd.